# Simon's Surf Glossary

**Off the Lip** Turning your surfboard up onto the wave as it crashes down.

**Cutback** As you're riding the wave, putting pressure on your back foot to turn.

**Duckdive** Holding the rails of your surfboard as you dive under an incoming wave.

**Backside** Surfing with your back to the wave.

**Frontside** Surfing facing the wave.

**Sitting Deep (Tuberiding)** Sitting in barrel as far back as you can.

**Pearling** While paddling, the nose of your board goes under the water causing you to fall forward (somersault) over the wave.

**360°** Turning forward or backward in a circular motion.

**Falls** The crashing part of a wave that forms a waterfall.

**Angling** Surfing across the face of a wave.

**Rail** The sides of your surfboard.

# Simon's Surf Tips

Make sure you can swim really well before you attempt to go surfing.

When you are in the ocean, always be aware of your surroundings; like waves, people animals and rocks.

Put lots of sunblock on when you're in the sun all day.

Never go in the ocean by yourself; always with a friend or parent.

There are a lot of activities to enjoy while at the beach besides surfing; such as boogie boarding, body surfing, swimming, skim boarding, volleyball, paddle ball, laying in the sun, hanging out...and everyone's favorite - building sand castles!

Don't be a litter bug. Always throw your trash away.

WHEN YOU CATCH A RAIL
AND FALL OFF YOUR BOARD,
MAKE SURE YOU HOLD YOUR
BREATH AND STAY RELAXED.

What kind of sea life do you see?

I HAVE LEARNED THAT WHEN YOU PEARL YOUR BOARD AND GO OVER THE FALLS, YOU HAVE TO MAKE SURE THAT THE TIDE IS NOT TOO LOW.

The tide is always changing. Even when we're asleep!

WHEN YOU DROP INTO A WAVE AND GO OVER THE FALLS, YOU CAN GET HELD UNDER FOR A LONG TIME. YOU HAVE TO MAKE SURE YOU CAN HOLD YOUR BREATH AND THAT YOU ARE A GOOD SWIMMER.

Can you count the bubbles?

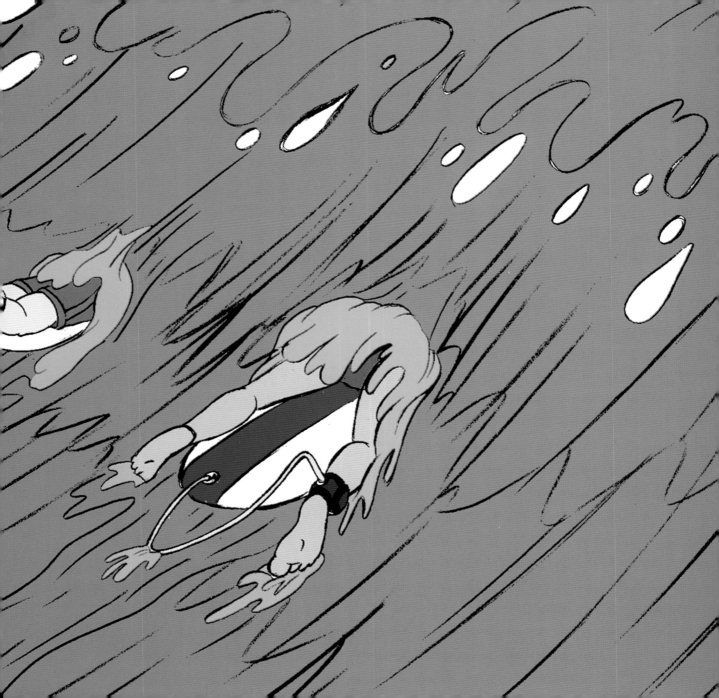

My mom taught me to duck-dive. As you paddle out, you have to hold your breath and dive under the wave.

The secret to duck-diving is timing and paddling strength.

TODAY WILL BE THE TENTH TIME I HAVE BEEN
SURFING. I CAN STAND UP NOW AND RIDE A WAVE.
IT REALLY IS THE GREATEST FEELING IN THE WORLD.

My mom is going to take me to the beach today so I can try out my new surfboard. I am so excited!

How many surfboards do you see? What color is my mom's car?

I HAVE MY OWN
SURFBOARD NOW. I WORKED
REALLY HARD TO GET IT.
I CAN'T WAIT TO USE IT
FOR THE FIRST TIME.

You should put wax on your surfboard every time you go surfing.

I'M GETTING VERY GOOD ON MY BOOGIE BOARD, BUT MY DREAM IS TO LEARN TO SURF. MY MOM SAID THAT IF I CLEAN MY ROOM FOR A MONTH, I CAN HAVE ONE OF HER OLD SURFBOARDS.

Do you do any chores around your house? What are they?

MY MOM IS A GREAT SURFER.
SHE CATCHES A LOT OF
WAVES, ALMOST AS MANY AS
MY DAD.

How many clouds do you see? What color is the water?

Saturday is finally here. I am going to ride the waves with my mom and my dad.

TODAY, MY DAD IS TAKING
ME TO THE BEACH FOR THE
FIRST TIME TO RIDE MY
BOOGIE BOARD ON THE WAVES.
MY DAD PROMISED TO TAKE
ME AGAIN NEXT WEEKEND.

How many shells do you see on the sand? What shape are they?

My mom gave me her old boogie board. I put it in the water and lie down on it. I paddle back and forth across the pool.

A boogie board is kind of like a soft and short surfboard.

WATCH ME DAD, I'M SWIMMING NOW! I'M ALSO JUMPING AND DIVING INTO THE POOL. BUT MY DREAM IS STILL TO GO SURFING.

Have you ever jumped into a pool? What was it like?

THIS IS MY FIRST TIME IN
THE POOL WITHOUT HOLDING
ONTO MY DAD. I'M NOT
EVEN SCARED.

What part of my body is making a splash?

WE HAVE A POOL IN MY
BACKYARD AND I CAN'T WAIT
FOR THE DAY THAT I CAN GO
SWIMMING IN IT.

What do you see out of my window?

SOMETIMES, MY DAD
LIES ON THE GROUND
AND I STAND ON HIS BACK
AND PRETEND I'M RIDING
ON A WAVE.

How many fingers do you see?

I'M CRAWLING NOW AND PRETENDING TO PADDLE, JUST LIKE MY DAD DOES ON HIS LONG BOARD.

A long board is a really long surfboard.

Now that I
can stand up,
everything I stand on
I imagine to be
my surfboard.

What color am I standing on?

WHEN I GET OLDER,
I WANT TO SPEND
MY LIFE ON THE BEACH.

Do you like taking bubble baths?

# Endurance Publications Inc.

*educational entertainment for kids on the go!*

Endurance Publications
POB 101 Agoura Hills, CA 91376

This book is available at a special discount when ordered in bulk quantities.
For information:   fax 916 482 7450
www.endurancepoblications.com

ISBN 0-9708805-1-0

Printed in China by Palace Press International/ Sabra Chili
Library of Congress Control Number: 2001089943

1 2 3 4 5 6 7 8 9 0

A special thanks to Azar Jahangiri, Marc and Lisa Sallin, Mom and Dad and every child in the world that enjoys this book.
Thank you all!!